ODYSSEY OF REBIRTH

CONNOR WHITELEY

No part of this book may be reproduced in any form or by any electronic or mechanical means. Including information storage, and retrieval systems, without written permission from the author except for the use of brief quotations in a book review.

This book is NOT legal, professional, medical, financial or any type of official advice.

Any questions about the book, rights licensing, or to contact the author, please email connorwhiteley@connorwhiteley.net

Copyright © 2024 CONNOR WHITELEY

All rights reserved.

DEDICATION
Thank you to all my readers without you I couldn't do what I love.

CHAPTER 1

This single event changed the galaxy forever and had the power to doom, save or kill all life.

When people normally say they used to be great, be something or even remotely important, they're lying. They really are. When I was in the Imperial Army fighting on a particularly hard world to pronounce (not that it matters now that it's a lifeless husk), I knew a man that claimed to be a billionaire, the best friend of the glorious Rex and even an inventor.

After spending three years with him in infected mud trenches fighting an enemy he couldn't even understand, I quickly realised that he was a liar, a nobody, a person who was useless and always doomed to die.

You see my name is Ianthe Veilwalker. I don't know why my surname is so weird and futuristic but it works and my parents loved me even as the laser blasts from their Imperial Masters cooked their brains alive. And I did have a good childhood and even when I was serving the Rex in the army I always fought to protect humanity.

That's how I ended up here.

I sat in one of the two corners of my black crystal prison cell that was barely tall enough for me to stand up in. It wasn't wide enough for me to do three steps in any direction and my legs were hardly short.

The entire prison cell was tiny and stunk of blood, corruption and charred flesh so I knew I wasn't the first human to be trapped here.

I had to admit that I really did like the small black crystal dome at the very top of my cell. I didn't doubt for a moment it was what my alien captors were using to watch me. The Dark Keres, the foul humanoid alien race that wanted to resurrect their God of Death, always liked to watch me.

I sort of got the sense that they feared me for some reason and they wanted me dead at all cost, and yet they hadn't tried to kill me just yet. It was weird and strange and I was glad they were next to useless at trying to kill me.

But today felt different.

It wasn't the normal hum, pop and vibration of the air that I now understood to be the life-saving magic that kept the Dark Keres and myself alive. But I felt like someone or something else was watching me and focusing on me like I was about to be picked for something I didn't understand.

Granted I could have just been going mad in this tiny damn prison cell, but that was how the Dark Keres won their psychological wars without even lifting up one of their magical fingers.

You see I had just decided that the Rex was a complete and utter dickhead that only cared about himself and corruption so I went rogue. Me and my squad mates decided to go wrong but the Dark Keres attacked us in our white pod-like shuttle.

We all tried to fight as much as we could but it was useless. The Dark Keres ambushed us and there was nothing we could even remotely do to save ourselves.

I was the only survivor and that was how I ended up in a damn prison cell waiting to die a death that I hoped would come soon. I love humanity, I love life and I want to protect humanity no matter the cost but being in a prison cell just isn't how I want to live.

Someone laughed behind me.

I stood up and noticed how one of the dark crystal walls that trapped me had turned see-through. I stared at the foul, awful Dark Keres with their almost translucent skin, humanoid features and burnt red veins that made him look like a demon.

He smiled at me but I could tell there was no warmth, interest or concern behind those eyes. There was only a lust for murder and pain and my death.

I instantly knew that it was my time to die but knowing the Keres they were certainly not going to make it boring at all.

As the Dark Keres clicked his fingers I felt a fog come over my mind and I collapsed to the ground as my world turned black.

Little did Ianthe know that on the other side of the galaxy a ritual was happening that would change her life and the fate of the galaxy forever.

CHAPTER 2

After fighting to protect humanity on hundreds of worlds, after killing more enemies than he cared to remember and after being betrayed by more people than he wanted to think about, Commander Jerico Nelson had never ever expected to be in the employ of the very alien race that he had unfortunately killed out of blind obedience to humanity's monstrous leader known as the Rex.

Jerico wasn't particularly a fan of this strategic position as he stood on the very edge of a massive blood-red crater with gentle slopes. The slopes alone with its near perfectly smooth red rocks made this a bad position to defend. Ideally he would have loved to be in a crater with steep slopes that would slow down the enemies. Yet these awful red slopes wouldn't do anything to make his defence job any easier.

The entire red, sandy, rocky planet wasn't ideal for defence. Jerico wasn't a fan of the massive red mountains in the distance that rose up from the ground like daggers, just waiting to kill him, his men and his alien allies.

He really loved positions that were surrounded by flat ground so he could see his enemies for miles before they actually got within striking distance. But he couldn't help his stomach tighten at the very notion of snipers setting up in the mountains to take him and his men out.

The only major benefit of this crater that was there was a small rocky platform that his alien allies, the Keres, had created for him and his men. At least that way if there was an attack then they could easily hide, jump down and use it as their own snipers' nest.

But Jerico just couldn't help focusing on the stormy sky above them. The blood-red clouds with small amounts of crimson swirled in them really didn't make Jerico feel at ease. The gathering storm looked evil, cold and like it was going to be the death of all of them.

The entire planet smelt of damp sand with the odd hint of gun oil, burnt ozone and charred sage from the ritual that the Keres were hoping to perform in the crater. That made the great taste of roast dinner form on his tongue.

Jerico stepped down onto the rocky platform where the five remaining squad mates of his were all playing cards in their black battle armour. They were smiling, having fun and acting like there wasn't a single danger in the galaxy.

Granted Jerico didn't know if the ritual was going to be attacked. He was simply wanting to be sure because the Keres, or as this cult preferred to be called the Daughter of Genetrix, were paying a lot of Rexes for the job.

He still didn't understand how none of the Keres fractions had any sort of currency and their society was based on need and mutual respect. But these Keres were nice, kind and helpful so Jerico didn't mind not understanding everything about them.

Jerico looked down at the bottom of the crater and just shook his head. The Keres were wearing some kind of strange bright white robe that made them look even more like elves and fairies, because of their pointy features, unnaturally thin humanoid body and their almond-shaped eyes.

They had to be finishing up the preparations because Jerico noticed there were the five red, blue and purple Soul stones that the Keres had been obsessed with for months. Apparently each of the Soul Stones contained a Demi-god belonging to their Goddess of Life Genetrix.

Jerico didn't buy it.

But the Rexes were good and he really wanted to upgrade his equipment and actually pay his men so he really, really didn't care.

"Commander we are ready," a Keres said in a scarily good impression of Imperial Tongue.

Jerico nodded and he tightened his grip on his machine gun and he gestured that his men should also start to get ready, because if an attack was going to happen then it was going to happen very, very soon.

Jerico watched his men go up to the top of the ridge of the crater and he was about to join them when he caught what was happening with the Keres below.

All of them were holding hands and sitting on the icy cold floor with sharp shards of rock digging into their asses. The five Soul stones were in the middle and they were glowing.

The Keres started singing a beautifully sweet perfect melody that made Jerico want to cry, something he hadn't done in decades and he felt the air crackle, buzz and hum with magical energy around him.

Jerico looked up and frowned as the thunder roared overhead. The violent storm clouds were coming together and Jerico had a very, very bad feeling about this.

It got even worse when an immense spherical warship belonging to the Rex appeared in-between flashes of lightning.

The Imperium was here and they were going to attack.

CHAPTER 3

I woke a few moments later and frowned as I found myself in the middle of a massive Colosseum made from the same awful black crystal as my prison cell. It was perfectly smooth, glassy and I just wanted to smash it up, ideally with the skull of a Dark Keres but all I could focus on was the strange ambition of escape.

The Colosseum was immense and I tried to focus on the thousands upon thousands of Dark Keres with their pale skin, awful humanoid features and deranged looks as they focused on me. But I could feel their dark magical energy crackling in the air.

All the foul Dark Keres looked the same as they raised their fists, their hand and their swords in the viewing platforms of the Colosseum. But there was one awful female Dark Keres that I could see and I doubted she wouldn't be giving me nightmares for the next few decades.

Her extremely thin humanoid body was

disgusting to look at as she leant over the edge of the viewing platform. Her was swinging her rusty sword wildly like she wanted to personally kill me, but it was her black rotting teeth that I couldn't help but focus on.

She was disgusting to look at. I didn't understand why anyone, human or Keres, allowed themselves to become corrupted by evil Geneitor.

I covered my nose as the air was filled with the horrid aroma of charred flesh, burnt ozone and another more alien smell that I really didn't want to identify.

I had always known that the Dark Keres loved playing games in their Colosseums, and this warband had to be powerful in their hierarchy if they had a Colosseum, but I could feel fear in the air too.

I flat out did not understand how I was now feeling things because this made no sense. I was a normal human woman that wanted to protect, treasure and love life but this ability to actually sense things was just weird.

"See what is about you woman," someone said in a deranged voice.

I shook my head as three human corpses appeared around me that hadn't been there moments ago. They were all former soldiers like me and they had been completely stripped of armour, weapons and skin as their corpses laid there.

At least I now knew how the Dark Keres dealt with their criminals. They simply killed them in the

Colosseums, and the bastards used this for sport and entertainment too. They really were monsters.

"Let us give the Dark Lord Geneitor," someone said, "a game to remember,"

I instantly broke out into a fighting position as I felt the ground vibrate and then a very tall Dark Keres woman appeared. Her white skin glowed dark and magical energy crackled around her.

She had to be a Keres witch corrupted by their God Geneitor to be a mindless instrument of his will.

I so badly wished I had a weapon.

The woman shot out her hands.

Black torrents of fire rushed towards me.

I rolled to one side.

The fire chased me.

The fire turned into dogs.

The dogs chased me.

I ran.

I couldn't allow the fire to touch me.

The witch unleashed more fire.

More dogs formed.

Twenty dogs chased me.

I spun around.

I had to fight death with life.

I charged.

The dogs hesitated.

I didn't.

I leapt into the air.

Kicking a fiery dog in the head.

It died.

Agony shot through my leg.

The dogs charged at me.

I punched them.

Kicked them.

Snapped their bones.

My skin burnt.

My clothes fused to my skin.

The witch made a black fiery sword form in her hand.

She flew at me.

She swung.

Again.

And again.

I ducked.

I rolled.

I fled.

Black magical energy gripped a hold of me.

Throwing me towards her.

I flew towards the witch.

She raised her sword. I grabbed it as I slammed into her.

I thrusted it into her. The witch died.

As soon as the witch's corpse disappeared, the entire damn Colosseum went deadly silent and they all looked to a particular point that I couldn't see. Maybe they wanted to ask their warlord what was going to happen next. Maybe they might give me my freedom.

I seriously doubted it.

"Most impressive human," someone said, "but let us see how you do against the most devout servants of Geneitor,"

I shook my head. "All I want is to live. Protect life. Save people. That is all I want so I don't want to kill you,"

I didn't know why I said that but it just felt right in the moment. But as a massive wolf the size of a shuttle appeared at the other end of the Colosseum I seriously knew that I could never ever reason with the Dark Keres.

The wolf charged.

I went to roll.

I felt a sword at my feet. The same one the witch had used. I grabbed it.

I charged at the wolf.

The wolf charged even faster.

I jumped into the air.

I swung the sword.

The sword shattered as it touched the wolf.

The Dark Keres laughed.

It was deafening.

The wolf chomped down on my leg.

Throwing me about like a rag doll. Breaking my leg. Shattering bone.

The wolf threw me to one side.

I landed with a thud.

I forced myself up. I couldn't use a leg.

The wolf charged.

I tried to run.

I couldn't.

The wolf whacked me to one side.

I smashed into the black crystal.

The wolf roared.

It was playing with me as it slowly came over to me and I realised that I was going to die here. I was going to become just another victim one of the Dark Keres and my soul or whatever it was called would be tortured and devoured by Geneitor, forever.

It was weird because all I wanted to do was protect people, preserve life and make sure that no one ever harmed an innocent person again.

I stared in utter defiance as the wolf came over to me and grinned with an unnaturally human smile as its fangs got closer.

The wolf snapped me in two.

CHAPTER 4

Jerico flat out couldn't believe how his protection detail had just complicated. He had no problem defending the Keres from the Imperium but he just couldn't understand why the hell they were here.

He was just grateful the crater provided a good position for all of them. But he'd be lying he didn't say there were a thousand different calculations running through his mind. He had to make sure his men were protected, the Keres were going to be okay and that the Imperials wouldn't be able to stop him in his protection detail.

Jerico went to shout to the Keres but his mouth was frozen and he felt like something was influencing him not to interfere under any circumstances. And for some reason he obeyed.

He rushed up to the top with the rest of his men.

"We have company," Jerico said.

He nodded at Thomas as he checked his pistols and young Allen looked unsure about his third battle but Jerico had faith in all of his men.

A deafening roar screamed overhead as a nuclear bomb was dropped.

Jerico wanted to scream like the rest of his men but he knew they would be okay for now. The Goddess Genetrix would protect them and as soon as the nuclear bomb touched the top of an invisible dome the sheer extreme impact was reflected.

Jerico's mouth dropped as he saw the sheer destructive power of the bomb rip the Imperial vessel limb from limb.

A Keres screamed in agony.

The storm clouds smashed into each other.

The thunder roared.

It screamed.

It screamed bloody murder.

Jerico's ears started to bleed.

Black lightning shot down around them.

Jerico jumped to one side.

The ritual was starting now and Jerico knew that it flat out couldn't be undone. Something was happening not in this reality but Jerico understood in a way he didn't understand that his life was about to change forever.

A furious roar echoed around the planet as Jerico saw two white pod-like shuttles were flying towards them. Some damn humans from the Imperial ship had survived.

Jerico clocked that the two shuttles were splitting up.

Jerico grabbed Thomas and Allen and he took them to the other side of the crater.

The shuttle landed with a crash and Jerico aimed his gun at the door of the pod-like shuttle. He wanted, needed to kill these humans to protect whatever was going on.

The shuttle doors exploded open.

The Imperial army soldiers exploded out.

Firing as they went.

Jerico fired back.

Bullets slammed into Jerico's armour.

He stood firm. He couldn't be defeated.

He fired controlled shots.

Bullets screamed through the air.

Smashing into the enemy's faces.

Heads exploded.

Skulls shattered.

Thomas's head imploded.

Jerico ran backwards.

More high-velocity shots screamed at him.

Jerico spun around.

There were snipers in the mountains.

Jerico ran over the ridge of the crater with Allen.

They charged at the soldiers.

Cutting them down.

Jerico unleashed the full power of his gun.

He slaughtered the enemy.

The shuttle exploded.

Throwing them forward.

Jerico slowly forced himself up and he was so

glad that he was okay. All the enemies in the shuttle were dead and that him and Allen could now go and reinforce the other position but the storm screamed in terror overhead.

Jerico looked over to Allen's unmoving body and he went over to it. Allen's eyes were glassy and cold and lifeless as Jerico noticed all the metal shards from the shuttle covered his body.

The storm roared overhead.

The wind was howling all around him creating immense sandstorms.

Jerico could barely see where he was going so he allowed his instincts to guide him.

He made his way round the crater but he was annoyed as hell he could no longer hear the gunshots and screaming of the Imperial soldiers. He really hoped that his men were okay.

He couldn't lose them. They had to live. Just had to.

Jerico found his way to the other side and he frowned at the three remaining dead bodies of his men. The other Imperial shuttle had exploded and the mountain in the distance shattered as a lightning bolt from the storm smashed into it.

"Help Genetrix!" a Keres shouted at the top of her lungs.

The storm grew even more intense.

Jerico ran up the crater.

Lightning bolts hammered the ground.

Jerico leapt to one side.

Then another.

Then another.

Lightning bolts were everywhere.

Immense chunks of mountain rock fell down around him.

Jerico ran away from the crater.

The chunks of rock hammered the ground.

And then Jerico went down the crater as fast as he could but he already knew it was way, way too late to save anyone.

ODYSSEY OF REBIRTH

CHAPTER 5

I wanted to scream, lash out and cry in agony as I felt my body and flesh get ripped apart but I couldn't. The pain was just too extreme, too much and the entire Colosseum became an evil blur of colour and darkness.

I tried to hear how the evil Dark Keres laughed, cheered and sang their foul happy songs in celebration of my death but the pain was simply too much.

And yet as the life drained from me but I realised that as everything turned white, that I wasn't actually dead yet.

I saw an immense picture of a Keres woman formed but this woman was kind, angelic and I could feel her sheer aura of life, hope and protection. She was inspiring as hell even though I didn't know her and all she made me want to do was get back to my body and defeat the Dark Keres.

"How badly do you want to protect life human?"

the woman asked in perfect Imperial tongue.

"With all my being,"

"Will you serve me and become the Daughter of Genetrix?" the woman asked.

I didn't know what she meant but I knew that Genetrix was the Keres Goddess of life, protection and hope. And if Geneitor was real then she had to be real too.

"Definitely," I said with such rage that I hope she knew how angry I was at the Dark Keres for daring to kill me.

"Then return to life Daughter of Genetrix and free me,"

Before I could ask what she meant I felt pure magical energy pour into me and I was flat out amazed at all the Keres knowledge, forbidden texts and divine guidance that was entering my mind. I might not have known everything about the Keres and their gods but that didn't matter for now.

I opened my eyes back in the Colosseum and I shook my head at the Wolf.

Everyone noticed what was happening as they stopped their cheering, singing and laughing. And let me tell you hearing that deafening noise stop was shocking as hell.

I thrusted out my hand and an immense white lightning bolt shot out that killed the wolf so quickly that I had to double-check that it had actually died.

"What is this?" everyone shouted.

I smiled as I felt the love, guidance and

protection of Genetrix flow through my veins. "This is the future Dark Keres. Genetrix has touched my soul, given me power and now I will make sure you fail to resurrect Geneitor and wipe out all life in the galaxy,"

"Impossible," someone said. "Geneitor is all-powerful. He has a cult dedicated to him and we will find all the Soulstones needed to bring him down,"

"You might have a head start on us. You might have the resources that we don't. But I am the Daughter and Chosen of Genetrix and I will not allow you to live any longer,"

"Kill her lads,"

I just grinned as the stupid Dark Keres leapt down over the Colosseum's black crystal railings as they charged towards me. I flicked my wrists and two huge white swords formed in my hands. And I was so glad I had specialised in sword combat back in the Imperial Army.

I charged.

I swung.

I sliced.

I diced.

It was a slaughter.

I ripped into the flesh of the enemy.

Throats were slashed.

Chests exploded.

Dark Keres screamed out in agony.

There were too many. Too many Dark Keres for me to kill. They would overwhelm me in short order.

I fell back.

I sensed the Keres were behind me.

I ducked. A sword passed behind me.

I realised I had to keep killing. Keep fighting. Keep living.

I didn't know how I knew. But each death brought me closer to my salvation because Genetrix would help me.

Yet first she needed death to power her creation.

I screamed in rage.

I dived forward.

Swinging my swords.

Slashing throats in bloody arcs.

Ramming my swords into chests.

Unleashing torrents of fire with my mind.

A sword slashed my back.

I froze.

The Dark Keres sliced my arms.

I dropped my swords.

The Keres kicked me to the ground.

They jumped on my head.

I screamed in crippling pain.

I unleashed a fireball.

Killing two Keres.

And that was when it happened.

I felt the veil between this reality and the next become paper thin and then they disappeared.

"Come to me Vita," I said.

An immense deafening roar, scream and shout in a language I didn't know all rolled into one echoed across the planet as a blinding white light appeared above me.

Vita was a demon, a demi-God, a creation by divine power that I could summon and I was more than glad about that.

She was a huge Keres woman with golden magical energy crackling around her.

She screamed out. She launched torrents of white fire. She unleashed all her divine power.

The Dark Keres didn't stand a chance as Vita slaughtered them. The Keres tried to run, tried to flee, tried to scream. It didn't matter as Vita cooked them alive, slaughtered them and scooped up their souls so Genetrix could protect them against the predations of Geneitor.

Within a few moments the slaughter was over and Vita just smiled at me, and I wasn't sure if this was Vita smiling or Genetrix. Maybe she was impressed with what I had done, maybe she was pleased to see her Will made real for a change or maybe she was happy that there was now hope in the galaxy that Geneitor and the Dark Keres might not win after all.

I didn't know what had caused this at all. I didn't know why Genetrix had decided on me as the perfect human or living creature for that now, to become part of her. But I didn't care because for the first time in my life, I actually felt like I had a purpose.

I had always been interested and dedicated to protecting, saving and helping to preserve life and now with Genetrix's power I had the ability to do it. So I bowed to Vita as she disappeared and then it was just me left in the darkness of a former Dark Keres world.

But there was a single rose that grew out of the ground, and that really did make me smile. It showed that even in the most deadly of places, life could and would endure and considering the thousands of Imperial worlds that had been rendered lifeless husks by the Rex's pointless wars, that gave me a hell of a lot of hope for the future.

A future I might not have been certain about, but a future I was really, really excited about because I was Ianthe Veilwalker, human and Daughter of Genetrix.

It was my job to stop the Dark Keres from resurrecting Geneitor no matter the cost.

And that meant the entire galaxy depended on me.

CHAPTER 6

As the storm screamed a final time and unleashed vast amounts of magical energy into the atmosphere that scorched Jerico's lungs and made him scream out in agony, Jerico collapsed to his knees as he saw what the hell had happened.

All the Soul Stones were gone now and where they had once been was littered with the corpses of humans and Keres alike. A lot of the rock inside the crater was charred and smouldering so Jerico had no idea what had caused that.

But he had failed.

It was Jerico's job to protect his men, protect the Keres and make sure that whatever had happened today was going to happen without a single problem. He was nothing but a failure.

Jerico had no idea how he was going to contact the families, friends and loved ones of his proud wonderful men that had died under his command. He couldn't tell the families any of the details because it was illegal for humans to work with the Keres but he wanted to help the victims of this attack somehow.

Jerico saw something move below him.

Jerico slowly went down into the crater with his machine gun ready to fire if needed. The entire crater smelt awful of charred flesh, burnt ozone and another strange burnt smell that was probably to do with the sheer amount of magic in the air.

"You live," a female Keres said in her blood soaked and blackened robes.

Jerico rushed over to her and held her in his arms. He applied pressure to the wound but it was still flowing too quickly. She was going to die and it would be all his fault.

"I'm sorry I failed," Jerico said.

The woman laughed. "You did not fail Son of Genetrix. This outcome was already predetermined by the Goddess and this has the potential to save or doom all life in the galaxy,"

"I don't understand,"

"Humans never do," the woman said. "The Goddess works in magical ways. She came to me with the last of her power a century ago so I could find the Soulstones and Rebirth her so she may walk amongst the stars like she did millions of years ago,"

"But I failed you," Jerico said.

"This is not the right time for Genetrix to return," the woman said. "And now know that I was not the one to Rebirth her. There is a human woman called Ithane Veilwalker, she is the true Daughter of

Genetrix,"

Jerico wasn't sure. Why the hell would a Keres Goddess want to have a mere human as her chosen.

"You must find her, protect her and keep her safe. She has just been reborn herself and you must find her. It is only through her that Geneitor is defeated and life in the galaxy will continue. Will you do that for me?"

Jerico nodded because he flat out hated the feeling of her warm blood oozing all over his hands as he failed yet again to save her life.

"Good," the woman said grinning. "Then take my necklace too. The Goddess was clever and she showed me the way. Take the necklace and may the Soulstone of Spero, Goddess of Hope, guide you like it has me,"

Jerico was about to question it. He couldn't be entrusted with such an important task, he was a failure, he was nothing, he was a mere human. But the female Keres died in his arms and he simply took off the golden necklace with the weird blue crystal at the end of it, and smiled.

He had no idea what the future was going to offer. The future could have been dark horrid and filled with suffering for all he knew but he had his mission and he had his destiny already laid out for him.

He wasn't sure that any human truly understood what intergalactic and maybe even interdimensional game of God and Goddess they were all blindly entering into, but that didn't matter. Because he was going to find this Ithane woman, he was going to find the Soulstones once more and he was going to succeed this time.

And bring down Geneitor once and for all.

CHAPTER 7

The thick aroma of smoke, charred flesh and death clung to the air as I leant against the icy cold white marble railing of the balcony I was using as my position. I enjoyed the small amounts of coldness flowing up my arms and into my soul.

The entire balcony itself was rather good for watching the surrounding forests considering it was a wide semi-circular marble platform used for academics, readers and other scholars. In normal times they would have read out here and studied their texts and ancient books in the bright sunlight.

That wasn't happening anymore.

I was completely alone on the balcony today and there weren't even any small crystal tables or chairs that had covered the balcony when I had first arrived a few days ago. There were still the little cuts, slices and chips in the floor where people had removed the tables and chairs, but they were so minor it hardly mattered.

The entire tower, or Library of Life as it was called by the locals, was a place I had always wanted to visit. The entire tower was created and handcrafted from a solid immense block of beautiful white marble with stunning gold veining coursing through it like a river.

I was even more impressed with the thousands of ancient leather-bound books that lined the white shiny shelves inside. I had never seen a real book before, most of them had been burnt and annihilated when the evil Rex had risen to power and conquered the Imperium.

Books really were special things to all of us remaining humans because we knew the key to our freedom and saving humanity was written in our past. The past that was burning down around us.

I smiled to myself as the taste of barbeques formed my tongue, my parents had always liked them with my siblings and our large family. They might have been all dead now but they had given me an amazing childhood.

A massive roar ripped through the air and I just shook my head as a bright red missile flashed through the sky smashing into the immense forest in the distance.

The sky was veiled in smoke, ash and little white pods called shuttles. I knew exactly why the Imperium was invading this world and killing my friends. They wanted to kill me and see what I knew about the Mother of Life.

I never realised that being resurrected by an alien goddess and being made into her Will incarnate would make me so popular with the monsters of the galaxy. But Genetrix wanted me on this world and thankfully I had a friend translating an ancient text for me now.

I felt Genetrix pull on my mind a little and I knew that I was running out of time. The Imperium would breach the world's defenders soon enough and then they would kill me and the knowledge of the text would be lost forever.

Of course I could easily open a portal and just leave but the text was too fragile to move and my damn translator wouldn't leave this planet. Some rubbish about their soul being bound to the world, I hated how magic worked at times.

"My Lady," someone said behind me.

I rolled my eyes as a Keres man came up to me. His alien humanoid features were perfectly thin, a little gaul and elongated. His body looked way too thin for a human but that was so common amongst the Keres.

Genetrix might have created the Keres to protect life and her evil husband might have created humanity to kill all life but they were basically the same in the looks department.

"Yes Tau'Koo," I said feeling Genetrix really trying to pull on my mind. There was something the Goddess wanted me to realise but I just couldn't understand at the moment.

"The orbital defences are wiped out and the ground defenders are weaker now. The Imperium has landed in the North and South of the planet and Keres lives are being slaughtered,"

"Damn it," I said. I might have been 100% human with the powers of a Keres but I had never wanted the Keres to die. They were good, amazing people that had to be protected, but my presence had brought the enemy to them.

I needed a new plan.

"How much longer does the Translator need?" I asked.

"Another twenty minutes at least but which-"

I waved him silent because I knew exactly what was going to happen in the next twenty minutes, this world was going to die.

"Then let us see what power the Mother can gift me," I said closing my eyes and connecting to Genetrix and letting her presence feel my mind.

I tapped into her power and started to course over the immense forest below me with my mind's eye like how a bird might fly towards a seed on the ground. I needed to find the leader of the invasion and I needed to buy us time.

If I found the Imperial leader that was threatening us I could find out more, I could find something to help us, save us and mean I could preserve life. I had to try. I couldn't afford for anymore innocent people to die on my behalf.

I scanned the battlefield in the distance again and

again and I was about to lost hope when I found him.

And I wasn't sure if that excited me or scared me a lot more than I wanted to admit. Even to Genetrix.

CHAPTER 8

Jerico flat out hated travelling on the run throughout the Imperium because he was never sure who to trust, what transport routes to use and what weapons to take with him. When he had been a military commander with access to all the official information that came with it, he had been able to keep up-to-date with security measures and other methods the Imperials used to kill so-called criminals (even though most of them were innocent people just wanting a better life). But he didn't have that power anymore.

Jerico was just glad the little rust bucket of a shuttle he stowed away on had made the journey to his destination. He had hated how the rust bucket had shook, vibrated and sounded like it was about to explode at any moment, but he was safe for now.

He wasn't sure how long that was going to last.

Thick aromas of alcohol, sweat and wonderfully sweet chocolate filled Jerico's senses as he went inside

The Lover's Bar onboard the disc-shaped space station known as Outpost-66.

Jerico smiled as he leant against the wonderfully warm grey metal doorway where a handful of people were coming and going. They were clearly military cadets judging by their cleanly pressed grey uniforms, and Jerico almost wanted to ask them where the hell they were off to.

It wasn't normal for any military units to be this far from civilisation, but he couldn't do that because he was hunted, keeping a low profile and he just couldn't draw attention to himself. And it wasn't like the military of the Imperium wasn't a massive Cult, if he spoke to the wrong person, then Earth would be told sooner or later.

Jerico shook his head at the very notion of Earth finding him.

Jerico hated how the entire bar was awful as a strategic position if anything went wrong.

The two rows of small metal tables pushed around the curved grey walls of the bar wouldn't provide any cover. But Jerico liked how people of all shapes, sizes and heights sat around the tables talking and laughing about their business. They were all drinking some kind of bright blue liquid that was probably strong enough to power small shuttles.

Jerico seriously didn't want to drink it if he could help it.

Jerico almost laughed as he saw three women in very attractive red dresses do some sort of exotic dancing on the oval platform in the middle of the bar. No one was paying attention to them so Jerico supposed their job was to simply get them in the bar.

But Jerico really didn't need them to get him in the bar.

Jerico went towards the massive bright red floating counter towards the very back of the bar. He clocked everyone was slowly looking at him, trying their best not to be seen, but he had been a Commander in the Imperial Army, he knew the signs of being watched. Jerico just needed to know how to find some forbidden information on a target and then he would leave all of these people in peace.

Most of them would hopefully be too drunk later on to remember him.

The closer he got to the counter the louder the humming, banging and popping of the space station got, it had faded as background noise so it was only now Jerico was realising the noise was still there. He still didn't like it, because it could easily hide the footsteps of enemies.

Jerico might have only been here for information but he knew how dangerous, deadly and isolating that simple task could be. Especially as he was outside the safety of the Imperial Military.

He knew from personal experience that if you asked any of the tens upon tens of trillions of humans in the Imperium how they would get access to forbidden knowledge, then there were only ever three answers. The most probable would be, they would simply report you to the authorities and you would never ever be seen again. The second answer would be you shouldn't because that is simply immoral and an affront to humanity and the Truth that the Rex lies about.

The third answer would be to find some kind of abomination like an alien, a historian or some kind of other forbidden creature that possessed such knowledge. The only problem with such things was that they were rarer than rare and you would most probably die in the process.

Thankfully that was not a problem for Jerico.

He gave the very tall woman behind the bar a friendly smile, but he was laughing more at himself than her. He just couldn't believe how obsessed he was with strategy and knowing how to win in a fight, he knew the skills were useful but they always popped up at weird times.

The woman smiled at Jerico as he leant against the icy coldness of the counter. The smells of oranges, lemons and grapefruits filled his senses making the great taste of lemon tarts form on his tongue.

"You want something that isn't alcohol, don't ya sweetheart?" the woman asked in a way that surprised Jerico. She sounded like she knew a lot more than Jerico wanted her to.

Jerico looked around the bar. All he wanted was a little information on where some human woman called Ithane Veilwalker could be, he had no idea what she really was. He was only going off what he had been told.

Jerico didn't believe for a single moment she was some woman who had been killed and brought back from the dead by some alien Goddess, but he had been gifted a task by a dying friend and he wanted to see it through.

"You seek someone," the woman said.

Jerico laughed and shook his head. He had no clue how to ask his question to this woman but he doubted she was as innocent or human as she appeared.

"I know if you want forbidden information then it is always best to start in the most remote regions of the Imperium," Jerico said keeping his voice as low as possible.

The woman smiled and nodded and Jerico looked around again and noticed a tall man wearing a black military uniform near the front door was watching them.

"Clearly I am not the only person who knows that little fact," Jerico said.

"Of course not," the woman said dropping her human-accent for just a moment.

CHAPTER 9

I kept leaning on the warm white marble balcony, more for support than anything else in case this human leader was able to attack me or anything psychically, as connected with his mind. He wasn't a good man by any stretch of the imagination but he was skilled in hunting, killing and torturing Keres. I didn't need alien magic to realise that because I could sense the crystallised magic of his former kills.

Even now I was surprised that if the Keres were tortured for long enough their bodies would discharge their magic and connection to their patron God in an effort to save their life. It never worked but it didn't stop the biological processes of the Keres from doing it.

"I see you monster," I said echoing the words into his mind and hoping I could force a reaction of some kind.

I felt his thoughts turn happy that he actually wanted this and he had been expecting this.

"Where are you abomination?" he asked, "and tell me, what thoughts can you see?"

I didn't like it how he knew about the mind-reading ability Genetrix had gifted me. There had to be a spy amongst my gang and that was a major problem.

I didn't stop though, I could see his past and abuse from the family that was meant to love him. I could see how the Keres had robbed him of the chance to ever see if his parents could love him (they never were going to but he didn't realise that) and I could see his name.

He was Bloodheart.

The name almost forced me to kill the connection. Everyone in the galaxy knew who Bloodheart was, I wasn't even sure he was real or just a myth to keep the Imperium scared. He was a murderer, a butcherer and capable of burning an entire planet for the fun of the killing.

I only needed another 15 minutes.

"You are an impressive name to find Bloodheart," I said feeling Genetrix wanting me to leave.

But I couldn't. I could face Bloodheart.

"Do you realise that you are not the only human touched by the Keres Gods?" he asked. "There is another one of you and he is strong, deadly and will kill all life in this galaxy,"

I killed the connection as I felt something stand behind me.

I instantly went for the long magical sword at my waist but I felt a hard knife press against my back.

"Tau'koo," I said hardly impressed that the damn bastard actually had a blade at me.

"There are many within your ranks that do not agree having a human as the leader of the Daughters of Genetrix," Tau'Koo said.

I laughed because he was no Daughter of the Goddess, even I could hear the death, corruption and sickness in his voice. He was not devoted to life, he was the Deathbringer, a servant of Geneitor.

"When did the Father corrupt you?" I asked knowing I could kill him at a moment's notice but I just needed answers.

Immense booms ripped through the air. Huge red flashes raced across the sky.

More missiles rained down on the planet. As did ten thousand little white pods. The ground forces were going to be overwhelmed in moments.

"The Father did not corrupt me. He showed me the truth about the galaxy and how humanity must die, the Keres must die, everyone must die,"

I snapped his neck with a single thought and whipped out my longsword as I went back into the immense library of Life. I was running out of time and I needed my answers.

I went along a narrow marble corridor with thousands of blue leather-bound books lining the shelves. None of them had been touched in decades but the hope of a better life and the magic within the pages kept the dust off them. Hope was a very powerful force in the galaxy.

After a few moments of going along the corridor, I just grinned as I ducked into a small white marble chamber through a small archway. There was a heavy wooden desk in the middle but my translator was dead.

Their body lumped over the damn desk and the ancient text was damaged.

I placed my hands on the translator's forehead, it was still warm and I hated the weird feeling of a warm dead body. It was wrong on so many levels.

"Let me see what never should be seen Mother of Life," I said quietly.

My mind was filled with curiosity, love and happiness as I entered the translator's last final moments. At least they were happy with their last task for the Mother. They were reading a passage about a Soulstone and they were murdered.

I shook my head because it was the Soulstones I was after. Whoever collected all five shards of Genetrix's being could resurrect her and then she could finally kill her husband once and for all. It was simple and I needed to find all the Soulstones.

I sadly had to push my friend's corpse off the ancient book and their body turned to ash and I clicked my fingers so their soul went to the Mother instead of being tortured by the Father.

There was a bloody fingerprint highlighting one particular section and I couldn't read it. The language made no sense to me because I was a human, not a Keres and I didn't understand long lost languages.

But there was still a little bit of hope.

CHAPTER 10

Jerico took a step back and really looked at the woman. She looked so human with her thin waist, fat cheeks and long brown hair that she should be human.

But after a few moments, Jerico realised she was an alien Keres. He noticed how her ears might not have been pointed but they had been cut to remove the points, her waist was unnaturally thin and her facial features were all too perfect, too pointy, too human to be believable.

Jerico instantly wanted to reach for his pistol on his waist to protect her. Everyone in the Imperium knew to kill a Keres on site if they were found but Jerico couldn't allow that.

He had murdered way too many Keres over the decades out of blind obedience for him to let another human make the same mistakes he had.

Jerico leant very close to the Keres woman. "They will kill you if they find you,"

"I know," the woman said. "That is why the Man In Black is here. He had heard of magical miracles happening in this sector, I heal people you see who shouldn't be healed, so he came to investigate,"

"And now he wants to kill you," Jerico said hating the entire damn situation with the Imperium.

"If you help me escape then I promise you I will help you with whatever you need. Yet I need to know the topic,"

"I need to know where is Ithane Veilwalker?" Jerico asked, nodding.

The woman reached down below her counter and started to look like she was mixing drinks of some sort. Jerico really liked the intense aromas of orange and lemon and grapefruit but she was clearly acting.

The Man In Black was watching them intensely.

"Ithane Veilwalker is a myth created by your Imperium to give us false hope. The Keres are dying and we are being slaughtered by your Imperium. We want peace and you people enslave us,"

Jerico shook his head as he felt his necklace (that was apparently meant to contain the Soulstone of the Keres Goddess of Hope, Spero) pulse warmly around his neck.

Jerico took out the necklace and showed its bright blue jewel to the woman. "If that is a myth then why is Spero wanting me to find her?"

The woman's mouth dropped and Jerico could see she was conflicted and awed and even in a little fear as a drop of sweat rolled down her hand.

Then the woman laughed manically.

Jerico took a few steps back and whipped out his pistol.

The woman's veins turned black, black oil poured from her mouth and Jerico cursed under his breath. She was a Keres alright but she was a Dark Keres. She had sold her soul to the Keres God of Death Geneitor, a divine being devoted to the destruction of all life.

Or so the bullshit stories said.

Jerico aimed. He fired.

Bullets screamed through the air.

The woman laughed as she ate them and her arms transformed into immense black talons dripping dark red rich blood.

A scream came from behind.

Jerico spun around. He saw men and women run out of the bar screaming and shouting warnings as they went.

Space Station security would be there quickly. Jerico had to find his information soon.

The Black In Man charged at Jerico.

The woman flew forward.

Jerico rolled forward.

He fired at the Man.

The bullets bounced off him.

Jerico leapt up. The woman swung her talons at him.

Jerico blocked them. He punched her in the face.

Icy coldness shot up his arms.

The Man fired at the woman.

She screamed.

She shot out her arms. Black fire engulfed him.

He screamed in agony.

Jerico fired at the woman.

Tendrils of black fire melted the bullets but then the Man's screams just stopped and everything went silent.

When the silent flames finished crackling and engulfing the man, Jerico gasped as the Man was just a skeleton made from black crystal.

"Kill him," the woman said.

Jerico fired.

A bullet screamed towards the skeleton. It smashed into him. Shattering the crystal.

Jerico scanned the bar for the woman. She was gone.

He carefully searched behind the counter. He could sense her foul dark magic here. She was alive.

He just couldn't see her.

Jerico felt his heart pound in his chest. He felt sweat drip down his back. He could feel his fear responses kicking in.

Then Jerico's chest filled with the warmth of hope that Spero provided him with. He calmed down and he closed his eyes.

He wanted to sense the woman.

Air rushed behind him.

Jerico jumped forward. He opened his eyes.

He just missed two immense talons.

He fired into the air but he didn't hit anything.

Jerico closed his eyes again. He couldn't rely on human senses to find a Dark Keres. He had to rely on instinct.

Air zoomed towards him.

Jerico leapt to one side.

He felt the intense rush of heat flow past him. He wanted to panic at the idea of almost being cooked alive so he didn't allow himself to.

The air churned around him.

Jerico ducked. Fired three rounds all around him. He kicked the air.

He heard a scream as a bullet smashed into something and then his feet kicked the Keres's head.

Something cracked and Jerico opened his eyes to see the damn Keres woman collapse to the ground gripping her stomach as black blood poured out of the wound.

Jerico pointed his pistol firmly at her head but he was surprised that she was truly smiling at him. Her veins had returned to normal and Jerico had no idea how these Gods worked but he almost believed she had been freed of Geneitor's corrupting influence.

If such things actually happened.

"You helped me escape Geneitor. Thank you," the woman said weakly.

"Where is Ithane Veilwalker?" Jerico asked.

"The Father of Death knows. He tracks her but he only allows me to tell a lie and a truth before he claims my soul,"

"Speak and die then," Jerico said hating that he was being mean to a Keres that had probably only fallen to such corruption to survive humanity's onslaught.

"Ithane seeks the history of the Soulstones or Ithane can be found in the grave on Earth," the woman said before she died.

Jerico shook his head. It was clear that Ithane was alive, his old friend wouldn't have sent him on this mission if she could be found in a Grave so it was good to know he was looking for some History thing.

But Jerico just grinned to himself. His next task of following Ithane in her search for History was going to be next to impossible, everyone in the Imperium knew the Real History of everything was impossible to find.

The Rex had rewritten history thousands of thousands of times depending on what he wanted his human subjects to believe, so finding the True History of the Soulstones and anything related to the Keres was going to be next to impossible.

But as Jerico left the bar and looked for a shuttle to steal (ideally one that couldn't be traced), he was really excited for the future because this was going to be a hell of a mission and he truly loved impossible missions.

Especially when they involved hunting down impossible information and sorting fact from fiction in the crazy universe that was the Imperium.

CHAPTER 11

An immense boom ripped through the library and it sounded like a thousand tons of marble had just come smashing down.

I was seriously running out of time but the preservation of all life in the galaxy was more important than my single life.

I closed my eyes and tried to reconnect with the translator's passing soul but I couldn't. Once a soul was given to Genetrix she kept an iron grip on it.

I just couldn't help but laugh because this was so stupid and I couldn't possibly fail but Bloodheart was coming here. And I had seen in his mind when I connected only moments ago, he knew the ancient language and he knew exactly what I wanted with the Library.

"Return to me Bloodheart," I said as I reconnected with his mind.

I almost jumped as I didn't expect his mind to actually be in the Library. He was here stalking the halls and killing the Keres defenders as he went.

"I was waiting for you," he said, "because I wanted to show you a party trick,"

I screamed in agony as I was pulled through reality and dropped off in front of Bloodheart as him and me were completely alone in the ruined remains of a library.

The white marble walls were smashed and the smoke-veiled sky could easily be seen through the immense holes in the ceiling. There were plenty of Keres corpses littering the ground and I wanted to slaughter him right there and then.

There were even a few smashed marble pillars lining the edges of the library.

Bloodheart in his heavy, thick metal armour pointed his sword at my chest and aimed a pistol at my head.

I went a little cold as I felt my connection with Genetrix fade a little and I just realised that Bloodheart was a son of Geneitor. I had no idea how a human had fallen to the corruption but I was still so new at this.

"You will regret your choice of Patron," Bloodheart said. "The Father kills and he will enjoy you,"

"I regret nothing but why this world? I have been the Daughter of Genetrix for three months now. You have not attacked me in the void, on Ferum or five different worlds. Why this one?"

"Because this world has Keres on it. I love

snapping the necks of the Keres as they sleep,"

"You are a monster," I said.

"I am what the galaxy has created me and I will help the Rex rule the stars in Humanity's name. No more Keres, no aliens, no more anything,"

I gasped for a moment as I realised Geneitor didn't have full control over him yet because Bloodheart still wanted humanity to live even though he had said the opposite only moments ago.

Bloodheart still had the weakness and mortality of a human.

He charged.

I thrusted out my hands.

Unleashing torrents of fire.

He flicked a wrist. My torrents went away.

He leapt into the air. Kicking me in the chest.

I fell backwards on the ground.

He landed on me. Kicking me again. Again.

The smell of death, smoke and rotting flesh filled my senses.

I shot out my hands.

Sending him backwards.

I shot up.

I flew at him.

Launching fireball after fireball.

He hissed.

He charged.

I charged.

We raised our swords.

We swung.

Our blades met.

Immense red flashes lit up the sky.

A missile screamed towards us.

I shot out another fireball.

Bloodheart hissed.

The missile smashed down on us.

I slammed my sword into the ground as the missile's explosive power was unleashed, I focused on my love for life, protecting the innocent and hope and a thin shield of dazzling white magical energy formed around me.

Bright flashes of gold, red and orange screamed past me as the deafening roar of an entire building collapsing echoed around me. I had failed the Mother, the Keres and ultimately humanity.

When the collapsing and the fire stopped, I closed my eyes and portalled myself to the top of the ruins where I simply sat on top of the very, very warm marble rubble. I didn't like how it was almost burning my bum but I didn't care because I was thankfully alive.

I hated how the sky was black with immense columns of black smoke veiling the sky. The forest was ablaze and all the little white pods were zooming back up into orbit because they had done their mission and I didn't doubt for a second that Bloodheart was alive.

The only sound of the entire planet now was the constant roaring, crackling and snapping of fires as they devoured all in their path. If there were members of the Dark Keres Cult on the planet then I wouldn't have been surprised if Geneitor was powering the life-destroying flames but thankfully they weren't here.

I just shook my head as I couldn't believe I had completely failed in my mission, then I felt my connection to the Mother restore itself and it felt happy.

A strange joy filled me as I realised that I wasn't just a human now constrained by the limits of a human mind. I was also a Keres with the power of a Goddess behind me, and I started to remember little passages and shards of information from the section of ancient text I had been reading earlier, that was all me.

But I understood it now and I just laughed as I realised my magic must have coursed its way through Bloodheart's mind when we were fighting and it must have found where he kept all his information about the Keres ancient language.

The passage the Translator wanted me to understand was that the Soulstones might have been bought together at one point in history. It was after all the ritual that tried to resurrect Genetrix failing at the same exact time as my own death that brought around my creation.

It was still more than that though, the book was mentioning how the Soulstones never wanted to be apart from each other and they wanted to be found. They would influence the environments, the worlds, the cultures that surrounded them so someone would eventually notice something was seriously wrong in a good or bad way.

I just shook my head because this was basically asking me to understand how the Soulstones had been discovered in the first place and then I could look for similar signs in the present. But the galaxy was a massive place, filled with billions of different planets and a Soulstone could be on any one of them.

I stood up and took a final look at this now-dead world I could sense that a darkness was coming here. Geneitor had a world to consume and he had a lot of dead souls to collect, but I was never going to allow him that for I might be a human but I am Ithane Veilwalker, Daughter of Genetrix and I am a protector of life.

I clicked my fingers and felt my connection with Genetrix strengthen as I collected all the souls on the planets and gifted them to her.

Then I swirled, twirled and whirled my arms about and I opened a bright golden portal to my flagship with my cult. I had a lot of reading to do, a lot of learning and a lot of things to think about because I was making progress and that was a wonderful feeling to have.

One day Genetrix would rise once more and then the entire galaxy would know the meaning of life and death. And only one side would win forever.

CHAPTER 12

"Impossible. The knowledge you seek is divine, forbidden and dangerous,"

Of all the sentences, Commander Jerico Nelson had suspected to hear as he sat down on a beautifully large golden throne-like chair, it certainly hadn't been that. He had wanted to come to the forbidden Enlightened Republic for the first time ever and he had wanted their help.

They were supposed to be the champions of Freedom, Democracy and everything the tyrannical Imperium wasn't, and yet they were still wanting to hide knowledge from him. Knowledge that might have been able to save everyone they loved and all of humanity.

Unless the Imperium finally launched an invasion of the Enlightened Republic and all of humanity killed each other in the process. Jerico seriously hoped that never ever happened, but it was only a matter of time.

Jerico just shook his head and he forced himself to look away from the ancient-looking elderly lady sitting at her oak desk in front of him. He liked how her long grey hair still looked full of life, joy and she was clearly healthy but she was just annoying him.

The entire chamber was actually rather good and Jerico really liked the beautiful yellow stone the high walls were made of. He wasn't too familiar with this particular type of stone but its shininess, strength and size certainly would have made it excellent cover to hide beneath in case of an attack.

Even the holo-art hanging on the yellow walls were impressive and Jerico was just happy he was here. The elderly woman might have been annoying, but this was the Enlightened Republic. It wasn't perfect but at least he could and probably would say whatever he wanted without getting arrested for simply disagreeing with the leadership.

"I will not give you any knowledge without permission," the elderly woman said as she stood up.

Jerico enjoyed the sweet aroma of roses, oranges and cloves that filled the air as she moved around, searching the immensely tall bookcase behind her.

Jerico watched her closely in case she was going to reach for a secret weapon or something. He seriously doubted she would but he couldn't be sure these days. He was already a former military Commander being hunted down in the Imperium for apparently betraying humanity.

He seriously couldn't believe the bullshit the Rex

had spread about him. He wasn't a terrorist, a monster or a danger to the very fabric of the Imperium. Jerico had only realised decades too late that the alien Keres they were murdering were actually great, innocent people.

Humanity was only killing the Keres because humanity was scared of their innocent magic. Jerico hated the Rex and all the idiots that kept him in power.

"No," the woman said to herself as she searched through some of her books.

Jerico looked around and he was only going to give her a few more minutes before he forced the matter. He was searching for anything he could get his hands on about the so-called divine objects known as Soulstones.

He didn't believe in the Keres Gods or Goddesses at all (which even he admitted was odd considering he had been gifted a Keres necklace that was meant to the Soulstone of the Keres Goddess of Hope, Spero) and apparently the Soulstones contained the souls of the Gods and Goddesses of the Keres.

But he didn't buy it.

And as much as he wanted to just forget about these damn Soulstones, Jerico wasn't going to fail his old (dead) friend for a single moment. His friend had sent him on a mission to find some human woman that had been reborn by the Keres Goddess Genetrix and he was going to find her.

That search all rested on him finding out about the history of the Soulstones.

"I need that knowledge," Jerico said standing up, surprised as the taste of orange chicken formed on his tongue. It was one of the most amazing things Jerico had ever tasted.

"Do you like the taste?" the woman asked.

"What is this trick?" Jerico asked looking round for any food he might have missed. There wasn't any.

The woman laughed. "I am Knowledge Chief of the Republic. There isn't a single piece of history that flows through the Republic that gets past me,"

Jerico really enjoyed how the sensational taste of fruitiness orange and fresh chicken got more and more intense.

"So what is this orange chicken thing? Is this some kind of knowledge?" Jerico asked, not sure he wanted to know.

"Of course. There was a tribe about three thousand years ago that developed technology to manipulate the taste of their enemy's mouth to disarm them. It was very useful before the tribe killed them,"

"I am not your enemy,"

"I do not know that. In fact there has been a full squadron of Death Troopers watching and following you ever since you alerted us to your presence,"

Jerico paced around. "Surely that proves I am no threat to the Republic. And the Republic has spies in most corners of the Imperium, you must know they are hunting me as much as they can,"

"It could all be a deception and come on Commander, when has a Commander of the Imperium turn their back on the Rex?" the Knowledge Chief asked deadly serious.

Jerico laughed, not because it was funny, but because she was absolutely correct. Jerico had no idea if anyone in the history of humanity had ever betrayed the Rex. He personally handpicked each and every one of his Commanders and they had to be extremely brutal, murderous and some insane things to grab his attention.

Jerico hated himself for what he had done. He had burnt entire planets of Keres warriors before, or were they all warriors? Jerico knew those planets contained families, young people and so many innocents but he never questioned his orders.

Because what does the lives of some alien scum matter?

Jerico just looked at the Knowledge Chief. "How do I redeem myself? And how do I prove I am no threat to the Republic?"

The woman only grinned and Jerico couldn't help but get excited because this was going to be a very tough mission indeed.

CHAPTER 13

"We're approaching Sandor now, my Lady,"

I smiled as my first-mate's wonderfully smooth, slightly high-pitched voice echoed all around me. His voice echoed perfectly off the brightly glowing purple walls of my chamber and I couldn't help but feel more and more excited about our destination.

"Thank you," I said into the air knowing full well that my blade-like warship's communication system would pick it up and send it to the bridge. "Send all the available data we have to my chambers and I want regular updates,"

I liked the warmth of my chamber as the purple crystals glowed brighter and brighter as the magic within them got excited about our destination. The air was wonderfully sweet with hints of honey, toffee and caramel like I used to have as a child back on Earth. I had loved those days with my family.

The lights in the purple crystals twirled, swirled and whirled around each other. and I had to admit, I flat out loved being reborn by Genetrix, the Keres Goddess of Life and Creation. I was starting to understand why she had resurrected me and wanted me to be her will incarnate. I loved life, I wanted to protect it and wanted to make sure that life endured no matter what.

It was why we were here after all.

A lot of my fellow Daughters of Genetrix, both human and Keres, couldn't understand why I had chosen a room so deep and dark inside the *Lady Of Light* as my chambers. I was her Chosen I could have made any chamber my domain.

But I might have been her Chosen, a demi-goddess some might even say but I never want the power of Genetrix to corrupt me and my purpose. So I allow my friends to have the nice places and this chamber isn't really so bad.

When I first came here the small box-room had smooth dirty grey walls and stunk of petrol, sweat and cheap sex. It was a small room that was screaming out to be loved, so that was exactly what I did.

Now smooth purple crystals line the walls and every single surface that it touched. I am surrounded by the quiet voices of the Keres and the other aliens and creatures that have pledged themselves to Genetrix. I can hear voices and Keres on planets on the other side of the galaxy, and I absorb all this information.

I'll never lie or ever dare tell anyone this, but it is a lot. It is so much information, so many voices muttering around me and I know I am barely able to maintain my sanity because of the amazing gifts that Genetrix had given me during my resurrection.

I focus on some voices for a moment talking about the Soulstones and I smile because that is exactly what all of us are searching for. It is why we were here and that is why I want to get down to the surface as soon as possible.

The loud hum, bang and pop of the engines filled my chamber as the entire fleet started to slow towards Sandor's orbit. I guessed we would be within launch range in a few minutes and the entire fleet would want to know my orders.

Sandor isn't the type of planet anyone normally visits. To say it's on the very edge of the Milky Way galaxy is an understatement, I wasn't really sure it had ever been touched by intelligent life until I felt the warm, loving touch of Genetrix correct me.

It turned out the sandy yellow isolated world had once been home to a small race of Keres. They were isolated, abandoned and they didn't want to worship Genetrix or the God of Death Geneitor. They wanted to be free, but that didn't happen.

The Keres on the planet were wiped out for some reason and no life ever returned to the world. And that is what I don't understand, the entire fleet and my entire network across of million worlds were all searching for signs of Soulstones, the shards of the fallen Keres Gods and Goddesses dedicated to life and the death ones. These shards were so damn powerful that they cause the very planet they're on to morph and warp in magical ways.

But Genetrix had led me to this planet and I have no idea why.

An entire bunch of purple crystals melted away for a brief instant as a very tall human woman walked in wearing some thick metal armour that I hadn't seen in decades. She must have looted it from a corpse somewhere, but her raven black hair certainly made her look good.

"My Lady we have completed our scans and there are no life signs. No signs of Keres's culture and no signs of Dark Keres too," she said, her voice wonderfully soft and careful like she was hiding something.

I could feel myself wanting to use my magic on her to find out what was wrong but I didn't. Everyone was loyal to me and I was happy that there were no Dark Keres about. I didn't need those foul Keres that worshipped Geneitor here.

"What else?" I asked stretching and I couldn't believe how great it felt to release the pressure in my aching muscles.

"There is a structure down on the planet. It's small, not very important but your name is spelt out on it. The structure is at least twenty million years old but *Ithane Veilwalker* is the name written on it," she said.

I grinned. At least that answered the question about why Genetrix had wanted me to come here, she wanted to find out why the Keres culture on the planet had written my name an extremely long time ago.

"No life signs?" I asked not understanding what had happened to the original Keres culture.

"Negative, but I suggest we get moving my lady. Our officers tell me there is an intense solar storm preparing to be released in three standard-hours,"

I nodded. That wasn't ideal because it didn't give me much time to explore but then again, that was the great thing about modern technology. I could leave it until the three-hour mark and simply escape the system into the Nexus and avoid the solar storm.

"Orders?" the woman asked.

I nodded. "I'll go alone but maintain contact with me at all times. And... something feels off, watch the other planets in the system and make sure there are no Dark Keres in the system,"

I could tell the woman wasn't sure why I was being so careful but no one just wrote a name down twenty million years ago on a dead world at the very edge of the Milky Way galaxy for no reason.

Something massive was going on here and I just had no idea what it was.

No idea at all.

CHAPTER 14

Jerico flat out couldn't believe the sheer darkness of the long tunnel the Knowledge Chief was leading him down. He wasn't a massive fan of the immense yellow sandy blocks that made up the rough walls with bright almost blood-red cement filling the gap between each block.

Jerico wrapped his fingers round his pistol just in case this was some kind of trap, but as much as he didn't want to admit it, he just knew the Knowledge Chief wasn't going to kill him or trap him or do anything untoward.

He got the sense that she needed him for something, a task that no one had been willing or stupid enough to do.

Jerico kept following the Knowledge Chief down the tunnel, listening to his own awful breathing that he was trying and utterly failing to keep under control. The more he tried to focus and control his breathing the worse it got, and Jerico just focused on the

Knowledge Chief.

He was almost surprised she was so confident, elegant and powerful considering how old she looked. Jerico didn't think she was wearing any technology or had any work done to her, but this was the Enlightened Republic. He wasn't too sure of the level of technology here, so anything was possible.

The wonderfully strange aroma of coffee, chocolate and strawberries filled Jerico's senses, making the delightful taste of strawberry shortcake form on his tongue, but then the Knowledge Chief stopped.

Jerico looked past her as a stupidly warm breeze brushed his cheeks and Jerico just knew that something wasn't natural about the tunnel.

Jerico looked at the Knowledge Chief who was grinning at him, almost like this was the last time she was ever going to see him. He was going to see her again no matter the cost and Jerico was going to survive this.

He hoped.

"What is this task then?" Jerico asked, not liking how the woman hadn't spoken to him for ages.

"This tunnel was originally created by the Keres when this world was owned by them. Then Geneitor unleashed a death curse on the world and there is a creature here that stirs," the Knowledge Chief said.

Jerico took out his pistol and shook his head.

"You might wonder why we haven't found the creature but the answer is simple. We have sent twenty men and women down here and none of them have returned. But I want to know what the Creature is and how to stop it from killing anyone else,"

Jerico nodded as he checked the sight on his pistol. "Actually my question was why build an entire human colony on a Keres Death World?"

The Knowledge Chief laughed. "Because only three people in the entire Republic know this is a Death World. Not even Supreme General Abbie knows this world's origin,"

Jerico wanted to argue with the Chief, because surely it was critical for the President of the Republic to know everything about her domain. But Jerico supposed that wasn't his problem, if the Republic relied on the same pack of lies, deception and falsehoods to remain as bound together as the Imperium. Then he didn't want to be here any longer than needed.

"I'll find the Creature for you but I am not killing it unless I have to," Jerico said not really knowing why he felt that way.

The Chief sighed and simply walked away.

Jerico went further down the hallway and enjoyed the wonderful warmth that flowed around him. He felt Spero's necklace pulse extra warmth into him and he knew this was a deception.

His footsteps echoed loudly in the hallway, a lot louder than they had a moment ago, and he could feel Spero trying to help him.

He still didn't believe in the stupid Keres Gods

and Goddesses but whatever the magical thing in the necklace was, it wasn't trying to kill him. Which he seriously appreciated.

After walking down the hallway for a few minutes and the wonderfully intense aroma of chocolate, coffee and strawberry got even stronger, Jerico stopped as he felt like he was being watched.

He closed his eyes for a moment and then he opened them to see a man standing in front of him.

It was clearly a Keres man. His long pointy humanoid face was ghostly white, his ears were like daggers and his massive grin made Jerico uncomfortable. It was even worse that the man was unnaturally thin even by Keres standards and Jerico couldn't see any weapons.

That concerned Jerico a lot more than he ever wanted to admit.

Jerico blinked and he found himself standing in a hallway that was three times wider. It wasn't natural but nothing about Keres magic was. He couldn't allow himself to die.

"I am not an enemy," Jerico said with as much authority as he could.

The Keres man nodded and he started circling Jerico so Jerico did the same. When the Keres man took a step closer, Jerico took a step back and vice versa.

"I am aware of who and what and where you are, but who am not aware of why you are?" the Keres man asked.

Jerico shook his head. He hated some Keres, they were just flat out weird at times.

"I'm here to find out information about Ithane Veilwalker. Do you know her?" Jerico asked taking a few steps forward so the Keres took three steps back

"Of course. The Reborn, the Daughter of Genetrix, the Unpure Keres. Of course I know of her the entire galaxy sensed her Rebirth and everyone searches for her,"

Jerico wasn't sure he liked the idea of that. If this Ithane woman really was as important to the survival of all life in the galaxy, then Jerico hated to imagine what the Imperium would do to her if they found her. Let alone what the Dark Keres would do, the servants of the very Death God she was meant to obliterate.

The Keres man took four steps forward so Jerico did the same backwards.

"What do you know about her?" Jerico asked.

The warm air crackled with black magical energy. Jerico aimed his pistol at the Keres' head.

"Humans, always so focused on weapons and murder and death when I have the information you need. When Geneitor burnt this world and left me alive to warn others of similar sins he gifted me knowledge and power and magic,"

Jerico aimed his pistol right at the man's forehead. "I have seen the gifts that Geneitor spreads and it all ends with corruption and death. Tell me what you know and I might let you live,"

The Keres man laughed. "Live? Life? I am a

servant of the God of Death. I do not care about life but now the Father of Death hunts you too. You have appeared in too many places not to be a threat,"

The Keres man screamed.

Jerico fired.

The Keres charged.

Bullets bounced off the Keres.

The Keres's arms became swords.

He swung at Jerico.

Jerico rolled backwards.

Jerico leapt up.

Firing his pistol until it was empty.

The Keres laughed.

The bullets screamed through the air.

Smashing into the Keres.

The bullets smashed onto the ground. They did nothing.

Jerico rolled his eyes. He hated this. He hated Dark Keres. Bullets were always useless.

The Keres leapt into the air.

Spinning around.

The air crackled with magical energy.

An invisible force gripped Jerico.

He tried to move. He couldn't.

His necklace glowed bright gold.

The Keres screamed in agony.

The force released him.

Jerico charged at the Keres.

Smashing his fists into the Keres.

The Keres hissed.

Jerico gripped the Keres's wrists.

Snapping it over his knee.

The Keres screamed in crippling pain.

Jerico whacked the Keres in the mouth.

The alien fell to the ground.

Jerico grabbed the alien by the neck and raised him over his head and smashed the Keres man over his knee. Shattering the Keres's spine.

An icy cold blast of air whipped past Jerico before he saw himself back in the same width of the hallway he had been in when the Knowledge Chief had left him, but the corpse of the Keres man was gone.

"He wouldn't have killed too many more people you know," a man said behind him.

Jerico looked behind him and frowned as he saw a floating skull. "What the hell are you?"

The skull laughed. "I must keep this short because I cannot control things in your reality for too long. But that Creature only would have kept killing humans whenever a human was stupid enough to enter the tunnels,"

"But the Chief Knowledge mentioned in passing these tunnels were sealed," Jerico said.

"Young adults, young couples and even the adventurous old always find a way into restricted tunnels so he killed them and fed me the souls," the skull said rotating to the left.

Jerico took a few steps back as he realised he was speaking to some sort of strange version of Geneitor, or at least that was what this skull wanted him to believe.

"You aren't Geneitor so go," Jerico said aiming his empty pistol at the skull and just hoping the skull didn't realise how empty the threat was.

The skull laughed. "And so my wife places the fate of the galaxy in a human woman and a man that doesn't believe in the Divine battle he is walking into. Oh this will be fun my love. Let the Games begin,"

Jerico was about to punch the skull when it fell to the ground and turned to dust.

Jerico couldn't help but feel like he was entering a war on a scale he couldn't even begin to imagine.

And he wasn't sure if that scared or excited him a lot more than he ever wanted to admit.

CHAPTER 15

After portalling on the planet, the first thing that struck me was the sheer silence of the entire world. It could have been because I had spent so long, so many days and so many weeks in my chamber listening to the mutterings of people on a million worlds. But actually I think it was because of something else.

After my bright purple portal closed behind me, I stood on dark yellow sandstone in the middle of nowhere. Behind me in the far, far distance there were some sort of mountains that looked like tiny yellow toothpicks set against the sheer flatness of the sandstone ground.

Behind me looked like a massive drop as if I was on top of a cliff-like structure, but it was what was in front of me that really captured my imagination.

It was simply a large orange stone circle. Ten immense chunks of orange stone were neatly arranged in a circle so perfectly that I doubted anything other than the Keres could have done it, so at least there was some limited evidence that the Keres were once here. I still didn't understand what had happened to them though.

An icy cold breeze brushed my cheeks and originally I had assumed it had come from the planet but as three other breezes covered me I realised it was coming from the stone circle.

Each breeze had a slightly different aroma but the scent of blood, death and decay was certainly growing more and more intense. None of this was making any sense because the Keres on this planet had forsaken Genetrix and Geneitor. I just don't understand why there would be any divine influence on this world.

I went towards the stone circle and I placed my hand on an icy cold stone chunk. I closed my eyes and tapped into my powers hoping they would illumine the situation for me.

Nothing happened.

Not a single image, phase or voice echoed into my mind. I didn't feel cold so I knew Genetrix was still with me but it made no sense why her insight wasn't being shared with me.

I suppose it was possible that even the Goddess of Life and Creation had her limits, but I doubted it.

I walked around the immense stone chunks and stopped at a small opening between them and I noticed there was an altar-like thing in the very middle. It wasn't made of bone, wood or stone. It was actually made of daggers covered in black oil.

There were letters on top written in the blood of a Keres that spelt my name, and it would have been the magic in the blood that we had detected in our scans. But I cannot understand why these Keres knew my name twenty million years ago.

I went inside the circle.

And the most intense wave of coldness washed over me as the golden light of Sandor's sun turned black, screaming filled my ears and a million voices laughed at me.

I clicked my fingers and my sword didn't appear in my hand. I was alone without any magic, weapons or divine protection here.

"She's here," a million voices said.

"She's going to die," another million said.

"She's going to become a Dagger," one single male voice said.

"What are you?" I asked channelling as much authority and power into the question.

The blood written letters glowed bright red and I went over to them. They rearranged themselves rapidly and I felt someone appear behind me.

I moved to one side so I could still see the constantly moving letters out of the corner of my eye. But I could still see the person or creature that appeared.

I recognised the twisted, demonic form of a Dark Keres instantly. The Keres were always beautiful, extremely thin and tall and just unnaturally humanoid in all the ways that humans could and would never be.

They had extreme agility, they were nimble and their charm was unmatched, but when a Keres fell to the God of Death all that beauty was twisted for Geneitor's own amusement.

This one was different though.

He didn't seem as corrupted and injured and mutilated as the other ones I had sadly met. This Keres was injured but his form seemed to be constantly shifting like he couldn't keep himself together.

"Who the hell are you?" I asked.

The Keres laughed. "I am ancient but young. Beautiful but ugly. I am your hope and your death,"

"Speak plainly or by Genetrix I will slaughter you without a second thought," I said.

The creature laughed. "How? You have no power Ithane. You have no magic, no help, no way to communicate with your fleet. They are getting very worried about you, they are scared, they cannot contact you,"

I shook my head as I realised this creature wanted my forces to come down here and look for me. The Creature wanted my forces here and I could figure out why.

"I don't know what you are but you created this entire situation to get me here. And I bet I can guess why. You knew I could bring you the chance of escape off this world," I said knowing that all evil aliens love that idea.

"Of course," the creature said. "When I learnt

about the Keres I learnt about your story. I spoke with Geneitor and Genetrix through their stupid prays and I learnt the truth,"

I screamed as I watched the creature transform into a perfect copy of me holding an oily dagger.

He pointed the dagger at me. "I learnt that you were the one that could give me the entire universe. Genetrix cannot hear you now. She will never know that I killed you and I became you. She will give me unlimited power and then I will kill her and Geneitor both,"

Fear gripped me. I had no idea who he was but for some reason and I hate myself for admitting it. I knew he was telling the truth. He really could do all of these things.

"And then I will conquer humanity, the Keres and then I will conquer all the galaxies," the creature said. "Oh those stupid Keres if only they hadn't prayed in their darkest moment. I never would have found them from my cave,"

An intense wave of icy coldness came over me and the awful aroma of death, blood and decay filled my senses. I forced myself to focus on the creature but my eyes watered and my vision blurred.

I saw him charge at me.

I leapt to one side.

He grabbed my hair.

Ramming the blade into my chest.

I screamed out in utter agony as the blade slashed my heart.

I gasped as he released me and I felt against the dagger altar with the letters constantly swirling about.

"I serve the Goddess," I said. "She protects life as I do, she protects the living as I do. I am her will incarnate and I will protect all life,"

The creature laughed behind me. "Say as many religious doctrines as you want Human-Keres woman. You will bleed out and you will die either way. The old Keres fell to my influence after praying to Geneitor so your own faith will be your death,"

I could feel my magic and life force drain away from me but I still forced out a smile and I noticed the letters started to slow down and form words.

"What's so funny?" the creature asked.

"I don't pray. I don't pray and neither do any of my forces and you forget something about Genetrix and Geneitor. They may hate each other. One may be the Goddess of Life and the other may be a God of Death but they will never allow themselves to be tricked by an idiot. They want to kill each other and they will never allow anyone else to interfere with the Great Game,"

The creature shrugged and I simply pointed to the brand-new words that had appeared on the Altar.

"Have Faith," I said as I read the words aloud and I ripped out two blades from the altar. "I believe in Genetrix and I will never stop serving my Goddess,"

I stood up perfectly straight as I felt the warmth, love and magical power of Genetrix feel my senses and body again. My stab wound and heart healed itself and I just looked at the stupid creature that had tried to copy me.

"You might be some ancient evil lurking on this planet trying to find a way off this world but I am not your ticket and I know you cannot survive in space,"

The creature's eyes widened and let me tell you it is creepy seeing your own eyes widen in utter fear.

I charged at the creature.

The creature tried to react.

It was too slow.

I rammed my dagger into its chest.

I rammed the other dagger into its stomach and I twisted the blades as the creature dissolved.

Then the bright golden sunlight of Sandor returned and I just smiled as I saw hundreds upon hundreds of small purple ships zoom towards me. My forces were coming and I was finally going home.

CHAPTER 16

A few hours later, Jerico leant on the massive oak desk in the Chief Knowledge's office as she just sat there looking, smiling and humming at him. She still looked as ancient as she did earlier but Jerico had to admit she looked good knowing he was alive and successful on his mission.

Her hair was still full of life, joy and looked healthy so clearly life in the Republic wasn't so bad even if the city and colony were built on a Keres Death World. Something Jerico fully intended to share with someone at some point.

"Do you have my information?" Jerico asked. "I need access to the Soulstones records,"

The Knowledge Chief laughed. "We don't have any records pertaining to such forbidden knowledge,"

Jerico slammed his fists on the desk. He hated this stalling, he hated the Republic, he hated how everyone was trying to stop him on his mission.

"Because the records never existed in the first

place at least not in a manner that humans could understand," the Chief Knowledge said.

Jerico looked around the entire damn office in frustration, hoping that there was a book or something he could grab or steal just so he could find some answers. But the entire silly chamber was just as good as it looked earlier with its beautiful yellow stone walls and impressive holo-art.

She really was telling the truth.

Jerico wanted to argue but he knew, just knew she was telling the truth. There probably were records available in the galaxy about the Soulstones but they were probably written in Keres or ancient Keres.

Something none of them could understand and even though the Republic protected the Keres as much as they could, Jerico doubted the Keres would be too willing to share such knowledge with them. Especially with the constant threat of Imperial spies.

"But," the Knowledge Chief said, "if I have learnt one thing in my long life about the Keres, it is that their magic runs on emotion and it is that emotion that will lead you to your goal,"

Jerico went to laugh but he hissed in pleasure as Spero pulsed loving warmth into his heart. And Jerico realised that he had a good idea where to find the Soulstones or at least find Ithane Veilwalker.

If he was a Keres God or Goddess (creatures that didn't really exist) then Jerico supposed he would feel safe on the world famous for where they apparently walked.

"Genesis," Jerico said. "The so-called Mother World of the Keres, the world where the Gods and Goddesses first walked on Holy ground,"

Jerico was rather impressed that he actually knew that, but he was fairly sure Spero had implanted some of the information in his head.

"And it is said that where their bare feet touched the ground ten thousand gemstones reaching to the planet's very core was planted," the Chief Knowledge said grinning like a schoolgirl.

"Bullshit, surely?" Jerico asked.

The Chief Knowledge laughed. "The Mother of Life has destined you for greatness but it will be a journey that will test you for sure. Now go dear Traveler because you will not be the only person to make this connection, darker forces now turn their gaze to the Mother World,"

"And soon another battle will be fought," Jerico said knowing exactly the sort of rubbish so-called mythic people tried to place.

Jerico nodded his thanks to the woman and as he went out of the chamber he felt pure excitement fill him because he was almost at the end of his journey. Once he found Ithane Veilwalker and made sure she was okay, he would have done his dead friend proud and he could go back to his old life of being hired protection and he wouldn't have to deal with anything more about the Keres, their Gods and their magic.

But he couldn't deny the chance of that was slim to none and that made him more excited than any guy had any right to feel.

CHAPTER 17

A few hours later after searching the entire fleet to make sure the evil creature was well and truly dead and talking to Genetrix to make sure I had actually defeated the creature once and for all (thankfully I had), I sat on the wonderfully warm floor of my chambers, cross-legged.

My chambers smelt amazing with hints of oranges, cloves and lemons and I was joined by three humans in white robes and three Keres in blue robes. Apparently there was some sporting competition going on later that human vs Keres and then later on there were going to be mixed competitions, which I always preferred, but right now I was in "Pray" with my friends. Everyone who swears themselves to Genetrix is my friend or to be honest, family member and I love them all.

But I couldn't help but feel like my ears were burning for some reason.

"We still can't find any Soulstones," a human

male said in a strangely thick accent.

"True," a Keres woman said. "We have to find the Soulstones if we ever hope to resurrect Genetrix to her full power,"

As everyone broke off into talking about their own theories, hopes and dreams about finding different Soulstones, I couldn't help but smile as I realised this was what I loved about my fleet. They were so wonderful, so dedicated and so committed to bringing about the resurrection of Genetrix so she could finally murder Geneitor once and for all that I couldn't help but feel proud to be their leader.

"I've found a Soulstone," a woman's voice said.

I waved my hand to silence everyone and I focused back on the purple crystals that were glowing intensely now. I clicked my fingers to amplify the voice so everyone could hear it.

"Report," I said.

"I am Leanne Oaks in the Enlightened Republic and there is a human man wearing a Soulstone around his neck. He says he is hunting you and he believes you will be on the world of Genesis. He has a Soulstone. We have to find him,"

"What is his name?" I asked.

"I do not know but he seems very interested in hunting you down. I cannot confirm if he is friend or foe,"

"Thank you. Continue your mission and may Genetrix guide you to your destiny,"

"And may she guide and protect you to yours,"

Leanne said before I closed off the connection.

"Orders?" everyone said.

I just grinned and I felt pure excitement fill my body because this was the moment I had been waiting for for ages. I finally had a lead on the location of a Soulstone and that meant I was one step closer to bringing my Goddess back to her full power.

"Tell the fleet to head to Genesis immediately. Summon all forces. We head there now," I said.

But I couldn't deny that the world of Genesis was a strange choice. I doubted the human man would have chosen that world because no one besides the Keres really knew about it, so why did the Gods and fate and destiny want me and him to meet on that world of all worlds?

I didn't know the answer but I was seriously looking forward to finding out. I was even a little surprised at why my friends here didn't question or argue with my decision to bring our entire fleet together, because it was risky as hell.

The Daughters of Genetrix had ships, soldiers and fighters spread out across the entire galaxy. I had a handful of ships hiding in each sector of the Imperium, I had a few hundred ships in mainstream Keres society and the Enlightened Republic allowed me to station ten fleets inside their boundaries as long as I was out of sight.

I didn't have a single problem with that arrangement and of course, I know it sounds like I have a lot of ships and troops and people at my deposable. I have in a way because Genetrix has thankfully touched a lot of lives, but it is a mere drop in the ocean compared to Geneitor's forces.

So bringing every single resource of mine to a single location for a single purpose, that might be stupid of me. I will secretly admit that but I have no choice.

This human man whoever he is has something I need to save all life in the galaxy, let alone the universe, I have to find this human. And it will take weeks to muster my forces enough to march on Genesis so finding this man is definitely a problem for the future, but I have to find him.

Genetrix returned me to life for a reason and I cannot fail her. Life has to endure and I will not rest until life is protected in the galaxy once more and who knows, maybe whatever happens next would to be explosive, deadly and a lot of fun.

Something I was looking forward to a lot more than I ever wanted to admit.

GET YOUR FREE SHORT STORY NOW!

And get signed up to Connor Whiteley's newsletter to hear about new gripping books, offers and exciting projects. (You'll never be sent spam)

https://www.subscribepage.io/garrosignup

About the author:

Connor Whiteley is the author of over 60 books in the sci-fi fantasy, nonfiction psychology and books for writer's genre and he is a Human Branding Speaker and Consultant.

He is a passionate warhammer 40,000 reader, psychology student and author.

Who narrates his own audiobooks and he hosts The Psychology World Podcast.

All whilst studying Psychology at the University of Kent, England.

Also, he was a former Explorer Scout where he gave a speech to the Maltese President in August 2018 and he attended Prince Charles' 70th Birthday Party at Buckingham Palace in May 2018.

Plus, he is a self-confessed coffee lover!

Other books by Connor Whiteley:

Bettie English Private Eye Series

A Very Private Woman
The Russian Case
A Very Urgent Matter
A Case Most Personal
Trains, Scots and Private Eyes
The Federation Protects
Cops, Robbers and Private Eyes
Just Ask Bettie English
An Inheritance To Die For
The Death of Graham Adams
Bearing Witness
The Twelve
The Wrong Body
The Assassination Of Bettie English
Wining And Dying
Eight Hours
Uniformed Cabal
A Case Most Christmas

Gay Romance Novellas

Breaking, Nursing, Repairing A Broken Heart
Jacob And Daniel
Fallen For A Lie
Spying And Weddings
Clean Break

Awakening Love
Meeting A Country Man
Loving Prime Minister
Snowed In Love
Never Been Kissed
Love Betrays You

<u>Lord of War Origin Trilogy:</u>
Not Scared Of The Dark
Madness
Burn Them All

<u>The Fireheart Fantasy Series</u>
Heart of Fire
Heart of Lies
Heart of Prophecy
Heart of Bones
Heart of Fate

<u>City of Assassins (Urban Fantasy)</u>
City of Death
City of Martyrs
City of Pleasure
City of Power

Agents of The Emperor
Return of The Ancient Ones
Vigilance
Angels of Fire
Kingmaker
The Eight
The Lost Generation
Hunt
Emperor's Council
Speaker of Treachery
Birth Of The Empire
Terraforma
Spaceguard

The Rising Augusta Fantasy Adventure Series
Rise To Power
Rising Walls
Rising Force
Rising Realm

Lord Of War Trilogy (Agents of The Emperor)
Not Scared Of The Dark
Madness
Burn It All Down

Miscellaneous:
RETURN
FREEDOM
SALVATION
Reflection of Mount Flame
The Masked One
The Great Deer
English Independence

OTHER SHORT STORIES BY CONNOR WHITELEY

Mystery Short Story Collections
Criminally Good Stories Volume 1: 20 Detective Mystery Short Stories
Criminally Good Stories Volume 2: 20 Private Investigator Short Stories
Criminally Good Stories Volume 3: 20 Crime Fiction Short Stories
Criminally Good Stories Volume 4: 20 Science Fiction and Fantasy Mystery Short Stories
Criminally Good Stories Volume 5: 20 Romantic Suspense Short Stories

Mystery Short Stories:
Protecting The Woman She Hated
Finding A Royal Friend
Our Woman In Paris
Corrupt Driving
A Prime Assassination
Jubilee Thief
Jubilee, Terror, Celebrations
Negative Jubilation
Ghostly Jubilation
Killing For Womenkind
A Snowy Death
Miracle Of Death
A Spy In Rome
The 12:30 To St Pancreas
A Country In Trouble
A Smokey Way To Go
A Spicy Way To GO
A Marketing Way To Go
A Missing Way To Go
A Showering Way To Go
Poison In The Candy Cane
Kendra Detective Mystery Collection Volume 1
Kendra Detective Mystery Collection Volume 2
Mystery Short Story Collection Volume 1

Mystery Short Story Collection Volume 2
Criminal Performance
Candy Detectives
Key To Birth In The Past

<u>Science Fiction Short Stories:</u>
Their Brave New World
Gummy Bear Detective
The Candy Detective
What Candies Fear
The Blurred Image
Shattered Legions
The First Rememberer
Life of A Rememberer
System of Wonder
Lifesaver
Remarkable Way She Died
The Interrogation of Annabella Stormic
Blade of The Emperor
Arbiter's Truth
Computation of Battle
Old One's Wrath
Puppets and Masters
Ship of Plague
Interrogation
Edge of Failure

Fantasy Short Stories:
City of Snow
City of Light
City of Vengeance
Dragons, Goats and Kingdom
Smog The Pathetic Dragon
Don't Go In The Shed
The Tomato Saver
The Remarkable Way She Died
Dragon Coins
Dragon Tea
Dragon Rider

All books in 'An Introductory Series':
Clinical Psychology and Transgender Clients
Clinical Psychology
Careers In Psychology
Psychology of Suicide
Dementia Psychology
Clinical Psychology Reflections Volume 4
Forensic Psychology of Terrorism And Hostage-Taking
Forensic Psychology of False Allegations
Year In Psychology
CBT For Anxiety
CBT For Depression
Applied Psychology

BIOLOGICAL PSYCHOLOGY 3RD EDITION
COGNITIVE PSYCHOLOGY THIRD EDITION
SOCIAL PSYCHOLOGY- 3RD EDITION
ABNORMAL PSYCHOLOGY 3RD EDITION
PSYCHOLOGY OF RELATIONSHIPS- 3RD EDITION
DEVELOPMENTAL PSYCHOLOGY 3RD EDITION
HEALTH PSYCHOLOGY
RESEARCH IN PSYCHOLOGY
A GUIDE TO MENTAL HEALTH AND TREATMENT AROUND THE WORLD- A GLOBAL LOOK AT DEPRESSION
FORENSIC PSYCHOLOGY
THE FORENSIC PSYCHOLOGY OF THEFT, BURGLARY AND OTHER CRIMES AGAINST PROPERTY
CRIMINAL PROFILING: A FORENSIC PSYCHOLOGY GUIDE TO FBI PROFILING AND GEOGRAPHICAL AND STATISTICAL PROFILING.
CLINICAL PSYCHOLOGY
FORMULATION IN PSYCHOTHERAPY
PERSONALITY PSYCHOLOGY AND

INDIVIDUAL DIFFERENCES
CLINICAL PSYCHOLOGY REFLECTIONS VOLUME 1
CLINICAL PSYCHOLOGY REFLECTIONS VOLUME 2
Clinical Psychology Reflections Volume 3
CULT PSYCHOLOGY
Police Psychology

A Psychology Student's Guide To University
How Does University Work?
A Student's Guide To University And Learning
University Mental Health and Mindset

www.ingramcontent.com/pod-product-compliance
Lightning Source LLC
LaVergne TN
LVHW011846060526
838200LV00054B/4182